AMBER BROWN
IS FEELING BLUE

Paula Danziger

AMBER BROWN IS FEELING BLUE

Illustrated by Tony Ross

G. P. PUTNAM'S SONS   NEW YORK

Text copyright © 1998 by Paula Danziger
Illustrations copyright © 1998 by Tony Ross
All rights reserved. This book, or parts thereof,
may not be reproduced in any form without permission
in writing from the publisher. G. P. Putnam's Sons,
a division of Penguin Putnam Books for Young Readers,
345 Hudson Street, New York, NY 10014.
G. P. Putnam's Sons, Reg. Pat. & Tm. Off.
Published simultaneously in Canada
Printed in the United States of America
Design by Donna Mark
Lettering by David Gatti. Text set in Bembo
Library of Congress Cataloging-in-Publication Data
Danziger, Paula, 1944- Amber Brown is feeling blue /
Paula Danziger : illustrated by Tony Ross. p.   cm.
Summary: Nine-year-old Amber Brown faces further
complications because of her parent's divorce when her father
plans to move back from Paris and she must decide which parent
she will be with on Thanksgiving. [1. Divorce—Fiction.
2. Parent and child—Fiction.] I. Ross, Tony, ill. II. Title.
PZ7.D2394A1h   1998   [Fic]—dc21   98-11233   CIP AC
ISBN 0-399-23179-X
5   7   9   10   8   6   4

For Mae Siegel—
a wonderful aunt

AMBER BROWN
IS FEELING BLUE

Chapter One

"Ta-da, dinner is served." Brenda, my Amber-sitter, comes into the living room. This week her hair is lime green and spiky.

I am lying down on the floor, doing my homework.

Brenda claps her hands. "Tonight I have made an amazing meal. I call it 'Mischief Night Delight.' "

If she thinks that this meal is amazing, that makes me more than a little nervous. Brenda thought it was perfectly normal when she made "Tuna Fish Delish." That had little chunks of celery and marshmallows in it.

I look up at Brenda.

She's wearing shocking-pink tights with a huge T-shirt, one that says PLAYS WELL WITH OTHERS. Mom and I gave it to her for her birthday last month.

I, Amber Brown, picked out the T-shirt.

I'm wearing the one my mom bought for me to wear when Brenda comes over to Amber-sit. Mine says NEEDS SUPERVISION.

Sometimes my mom thinks that she's very funny.

I get up, and we go into the kitchen.

Brenda has the table all set. "It's the Mischief Night menu."

I look at the table. In the center, there is chili made with ground meat. In the middle of the meat, on top, she has placed two gumballs, which look like eyes.

Avocado halves are filled with green Jell-O.

She's even used the plastic pumpkin that my mom will fill tomorrow with the candy that we're giving out for Halloween. It's filled with cauliflower.

"It looks like the pumpkin's brains. Isn't that cool?" Brenda looks pleased with herself.

The cauliflower is steaming and looks very squishy, and there's tomato sauce poured over it to look like blood.

"Yum," Brenda says.

I just look at it.

"Yum," Brenda repeats.

Brenda pretends to be the waiter and pulls out my chair.

I sit down.

She pretends to read from a menu, even though it is actually a serving spoon. "What would you like to order from our liquid list? Our milk is a very good year."

I laugh.

Whenever I see someone in a movie ordering wine, the waiter always says things like "This is a very good year."

Somehow I don't think old milk would be too delicious.

"Actually, the milk is a very good *week* . . . this one," Brenda says.

"Fine." I look at the meal. "Then I will have a glass of milk. Which milk, do you think, goes better with this food? Chocolate? Vanilla?"

"Might I suggest the strawberry? It would look good with the orange of the pump-kin, the brown of the meat, the red of the pumpkin blood," Brenda says, going over to the blender and putting in some milk and some strawberries.

We sit down to eat.

I stare at the meal but don't eat anything.

"It won't kill you. I promise." Brenda starts eating. "Yum."

Brenda said "Yum" the time she ate the tuna-and-marshmallow meal. THAT was definitely not a "Yum" meal.

I take a tiny taste of each thing.

It is an amazing meal. What is amazing is that it tastes good.

"So, what are you going to wear tomor-row for Halloween?" I ask.

Brenda smiles. "For Halloween, I'm going to dress 'normal.' I'm going to wear a wig that is a normal color and has a normal bor-ing cut. And I'm going to wear one of my mother's normal dresses and a pair of heels. That will be my costume."

I tell her what I'm going to wear even though I'm keeping it a secret from everyone else. No one else will know until tomorrow.

"So," she says, changing the subject, "when is your dad moving back here from Paris?

"In just two weeks." I clap my hands. "I can't wait."

Brenda grins at me. "You are so excited. Tell me about your dad." Because Brenda became my Amber-sitter after my parents divorced, after my dad moved to Paris, she's never met him.

I describe my dad. "He's not real skinny. He's not real fat. . . . He's got a real nice smile when he's happy. . . . Sometimes he tells very corny jokes. . . . He's losing his hair . . . only when I tell him that, he says that it's not lost, that it's just flown off in a hairplane."

Brenda smiles. "He sounds funny."

I nod. "He is . . . or, he was. I've only seen him twice since he moved to Paris . . . once in England . . . and a couple of weeks ago, when he came back to see about his new job . . . and to see ME. But we talk on the phone all the time, and he says that when he moves back, he's going to spend a lot of time with me . . . he's going to take me on trips, to the movies, to lots of places . . . and when he gets an apartment, it's going to have two bedrooms so that I will always have a place to stay with him. And I can pick out all new furniture and decorate it the way I want."

"Cool." Brenda takes a sip of her strawberry milk. "You're so lucky."

I look at Brenda and think about how she has no father because he was killed in a car crash almost a year ago, before I knew her.

She looks sad.

I reach over and pat her on her hand. "When Dad moves back, I'm going to ask him if you can do some stuff with us . . . not as my Amber-sitter, but as my friend."

Brenda puts her hand on top of mine. "If I had a sister, I'd want her to be just like you."

"Me too," I say. "If I had a sister, I'd want her to be just like you."

I pat her hand again and then stand up. "I've got to get something. I'll be right back."

Running up the stairs to my room, I open my closet door, and take a box off the top shelf.

I haven't shown it to anyone else yet. It's like it was my own little secret, my own little private special thing.

There's no way I can show it to my mom.

I don't think she's going to like it.

There's no way I can show it to Max, the guy my mom is going to marry.

I don't think he's going to like it either. I think he's gotten used to being the only grown-up guy in my everyday life.

Rushing down the steps with it, I put the box on the table, and open it up.

Inside is the "Countdown to Dad" book, which I got in the mail last week.

My dad made it for me.

It's made out of construction paper and has four pages.

The first is the cover. On it, he's written "Countdown to Dad" and drawn lots of hearts.

The other three pages are made up to look like a weekly calendar, with numbered squares. The numbers go from twenty-one to zero. In each square is a picture of Dad and me. There's also a tiny box where I can check off each day when it's over. The first

photo is of the day when he and Mom brought me home from the hospital when I was a baby. Mom took that picture (and most of the others). The rest of the pictures also show Dad and me together. As the countdown goes on, I get older and Dad gets balder. The next-to-last picture is labeled "One more day until I'm back and can hug my little girl." It's a picture that Aunt Pam took of my dad and me when we were in London. I have chicken-pox scabs on my face. The last picture is one that Brandi took of my dad and me at the bowling alley, when he was here to visit and work out moving back.

On the "Zero Square," he's written "Reunion" and he's drawn more hearts.

Only fourteen more days to check off. . . . I can't wait.

Chapter
Two

I, Amber Brown, have just seen a ghost.

Actually, I've just seen three ghosts.

Actually, I've just seen three ghosts, two werewolves, fourteen superheroes, five princesses, one devil, seven skeletons, six headless people, and a partridge in a pear tree.

I, Amber Brown, am dressed as a crayon and am handing out Halloween candy.

After school, my friend Brandi and I did our trick-or-treating, and I got three bags of stuff. So now I'm helping my mom hand out treats, and I'm still wearing my crayon costume, the one that I made all by myself.

When I was growing up, I hated my name, hated being teased about being the shade of a crayon, and I never would have dressed as a crayon.

Now that I'm in fourth grade, I, Amber Brown, am proud of my name.

It's a very colorful name for a very colorful person. . . . That's what my mom always tells me. I like having a unique name, one that no one else has. That's why I made my costume.

I forget what I'm wearing and start to sit down on the sofa. It doesn't work.

The only problem with being dressed as a crayon is that it is very hard to sit down and it's a pain to keep taking it off so for the past four hours I've been standing. Actually, there is another problem about being dressed as a crayon, but I don't want to talk about it because it has to do with trying to go to the bathroom.

I, Amber Brown, am one very tired crayon.

I'm also a very full crayon, having eaten lots of things from my own trick-or-treating and from what we're giving away: candy corn, Tootsie Rolls, and Fruit Roll-Ups.

We're also giving away some of the stuff that I got when I went trick-or-treating, things like granola bars and packages of trail mix.

The doorbell rings.

It's someone dressed as a pizza man.

He's wearing the uniform and a mask.

He's also carrying a pizza box.

I, Amber Brown, can smell pizza, real pizza.

I know that smell a mile away.

Either the pizza man is carrying real hot pizza or he's wearing a cologne that smells like pizza.

Maybe when I grow up that's what I should give my friend Justin, who moved away . . . . eau de pizza. Justin would probably like eau de pizza with pepperoni . . . . but without anchovies.

"TREAT. . . . NO TRICK," the pizza man yells out.

I know that voice.

It's Max.

My mom walks into the room.

She's dressed as a Halloween pumpkin, wearing a huge orange sweatshirt with one of those paper-accordionlike pumpkins on her head. It's a little embarrassing to see my own mother dressed like that, but at least she's not wearing it outside, where my friends can see her.

"Now, that is what I call a treat." She grins.

Max hands me the box of pizza and goes over to her.

They hug and kiss.

Then they look at each other and laugh.

Then they hug and kiss again.

"Cut the mush," I yell.

They turn and look at me.

Max walks over, picks me up sideways, and pretends to be writing on the wall as if I really am a crayon.

"I LOVE YOU, SARAH AND AMBER," he says, spelling out the words.

The way he moves me is making me a little sick . . . . especially at the O, the U, and the B. It's either that or all the candy corn, the Tootsie Rolls, and the Fruit Roll-Ups . . . . that, plus the fact that I haven't gone to the bathroom since I've put the costume on.

Max puts me down.

I make sure that my costume is still OK.

Max and my mother make sure that their lips can still magnetize to each other's.

It's still a little weird to see Mom and Max kiss.

Even though my mom and my dad didn't kiss very much when they were still married, at least not in front of me, it makes me a little embarrassed to see Mom and Max liplock.

I can feel myself blush.

Maybe on my crayon I should change the name of the color from Amber Brown to Cherry Red.

I go over to Mom and Max and step on their toes.

"TRICK OR TREAT," I say, holding the pizza box.

Max grins. "I'm the one who should be saying 'trick or treat.' Just wait until I tell you what I have planned for us to do."

Chapter Three

I, Amber Brown, feel like a wax crayon that is beginning to melt.

I take off my costume and rush to the bathroom.

Life as a noncrayon is much easier than life as a crayon.

When I return, my mom is opening the pizza box.

"Yum," she says.

Glup, I think.

I'm so full from all the candy that I've eaten, I bet I can't eat a thing. It's pizza with black olives.

I, Amber Brown, have developed a taste for black olives.

My stomach feels like there is a small place in it where the pizza can fit.

I quickly decide which piece has the most black olives on it and pick that one up.

I wonder what pizza with candy corn would taste like.

I take some out of my pocket and put it on my slice, hoping no one notices.

"Amber, I know that the food gets mixed up in your stomach, but the candy corn on your pizza looks repulsive." My mom shakes her head.

"Thank you," I say, licking the cheese off one of the corns and putting some of the candy on the table. "It's a new recipe. Try it."

Max puts a few pieces on his slice.

My mother makes a face and doesn't try it.

"I just spoke to Alice," Max says.

"How is she?" my mom asks.

"Who is she?" I ask.

"Alice is my sister." Max takes a bite of his pizza and says, "Amber, honey, I don't think that candy corn is going to catch on as a new topping."

Alice. She's the person who changed my life and my mom's life. When she worked with Mom, she introduced her to Max, and then she moved away. I don't think that she moved because she was nervous about what if they didn't like each other and blamed her. But I don't know for sure, because she moved away while I was in England with my Aunt Pam.

Max continues, "She's not very happy now. She and Bob broke up, and she really doesn't know many people in Walla Walla, and she doesn't like her job."

Walla Walla. I wonder if anyone can say the name of that place without smiling. Walla Walla.

"She'd love to leave," Max continues, "but Jade's just gotten used to the move and her new school. So she's going to stay until the end of the school year. She can save up some money and decide then. She didn't want me to help out with the move right now."

I wonder what Max's plan is, what the treat is going to be. I also wonder if all of this talk about Alice, Jade, and Walla Walla has anything to do with Max's treat. Mom is always telling me that I have to learn to be patient and listen and wait. So I, Amber Brown, am trying to be patient and listen and wait. That's not always easy.

I think about how Jade's name is also a color.

Then I think about how no one else should have been given the name of a color after I was born.

I, Amber Brown, really like being original.

At least Jade doesn't have two names that are each a color and together make still another color.

Max and Mom start talking about how neither of them ever liked Bob, whom Alice had dated for only about six months before they moved to Walla Walla.

I'm glad that Max and Mom didn't do anything like that.

I'm glad that they're waiting for a while to get married. I, Amber Brown, don't think I can go through another breakup.

It was awful when my parents split up.

It would kill me if Mom and Max did split up . . . . . unless it means that when my dad moves back from Paris, my parents make up and get back together again.

I don't think that's going to happen, though, and if it did, it would probably be a disaster. And if my mom and dad did get back together, what would happen to Max? I can't imagine not having him in my life.

I think about Jade, Alice's six-year-old, and feel bad for her. Her father leaves before she's born, never comes back, and never gets in touch.

My dad went to Paris to work, but he's always in touch, and he's coming back.

And Max cares about me, too.

I feel bad for Jade.

"So, Amber, what do you think?" Mom asks.

I don't want to tell her that I've been thinking about lots of stuff, especially that

I was thinking about my dad and I was not listening to their conversation. I just shrug.

"Amber," Mom says, "don't you want to go to Walla Walla for Thanksgiving? Won't that be fun?"

I, Amber Brown, am very surprised.

Walla Walla for Thanksgiving . . .

"Where is Walla Walla?" I ask.

"Washington . . . the state," Mom informs me.

Walla Walla, Washington . . . . *That's so far away,* I think. That's also a lot of W's.

We have only four days off from school.

"How are we going to get there? Where will we stay? Will Mom still make her sweet potato pie?" I love my mom's sweet potato pie.

Max answers: "I'll buy the plane tickets. We'll leave right after school ends. There's a flight that leaves from Newark airport. We'll arrive late in Walla Walla . . . . but, remember, there is a time difference between Newark and Washington State, so it won't seem so late."

"And when we get there, we'll bake the pie together." Mom smiles at me.

I smile back.

The doorbell rings.

There are four skeletons, one Easter bunny, two Munchkins, a Dorothy, and Toto at our door.

I give them candy, pop a Tootsie Roll into my mouth, and go back into the dining room.

The doorbell rings again.

This time my mother goes to the door.

Max says, "So, Amber, it'll be fun . . . . don't you think so? A trip across the country . . . . a new place to visit . . . and I really want you to meet my sister and Jade. After all, we're all going to be family soon. We're practically family now."

I think about it.

I bet that any sister of Max's is fun, and I'll be going someplace I've never been before.

My mother walks back into the room. "I just left a large bowl of candy outside the door, with a note saying, 'Please do not disturb us. We're having dinner. . . . . So just take one piece of candy each.' "

I, Amber Brown, giggle.

Sometimes my mom is so funny.

28

She actually believes that kids will take just one piece of candy each.

Max and Mom look at me, waiting for my answer.

I've never been away from home for Thanksgiving. It's always been at our house.

I think about it.

I've never been to Walla Walla, Washington.

It might be fun.

"Oh, OK." I grin. "I wanna wanna go to Walla Walla."

Mom and Max smile and start making plans.

I eat another piece of pizza and sit for a minute to see if my stomach is going to explode. Then I go out to the porch and check and see if there is anything left in the candy bowl.

There is.

Only it's not the candy we left out. That's all gone.

People have made trades.

In the bowl are five apples, three boxes of raisins, one half-eaten Bit-O-Honey, and two granola bars.

Trick or treat.

Chapter
Four

I, Amber Brown, have overslept.

I, Amber Brown, have a mother who has overslept.

Maybe too much candy corn can cause a person not to wake up on time in the morning. But my mom didn't eat candy corn, and she still didn't come into my room and wake me up until 9:00 A.M.

Maybe her excuse is that she stayed up late, talking with Max. I know that he didn't leave until after midnight . . . and the reason I know that is because I was awake in bed, looking at "Countdown to Dad," read-

31

ing a book under the covers, and eating candy corn.

I, Amber Brown, don't think that I want to see another piece of candy corn until next Halloween.

"Amber, get up. We've got to rush." My mother sticks her head back into my room.

Actually, she sticks her head and part of her body back into the room. I never understand why people say that someone sticks a head into a room . . . . and why the neck . . . . and shoulders . . . . are never mentioned. It seems so weird to think of just a head coming into the room.

I think that the combination of Halloween, candy corn, reading, and not going to sleep until after midnight is getting to me . . . . that, and my very active imagination.

"Amber, move it," my mother says in a voice that really says "Move it . . . . and I mean NOW."

I "move it" immediately, jumping out of bed, taking off my pajamas, and quickly putting on clothes.

I rush down the steps.

Mom puts a peanut butter sandwich in my mouth and hands me a glass of orange juice. "I'll give you the money for lunch. Let's go. I've got a major meeting in forty-five minutes."

Quickly I eat, grab my knapsack, put some candy corn into it (just in case I change my mind about not having any until next Halloween), and rush out to the car.

Mom gets into the car and says, "Seat belt on."

While we ride to school, my mom keeps talking about how late we both are and how excited she is that we're all going to Walla Walla.

I think about how late we both are, how much fun it will be to fly to Walla Walla on Thanksgiving, and how gross it is that I forgot to brush my teeth . . . . and my hair.

Borrowing Mom's hairbrush, I try to get my hair to look good, or at least not to look like one of those dumb troll dolls.

It's too hard to think straight this early, I mean, late, in the morning . . . when we've overslept and I'm late for school . . . and my breath smells and I look like a troll doll.

I hold my hand over my mouth so that the air goes up and my nose can smell my breath.

It smells of candy corn, peanut butter, and morning mouth.

I wonder if I can get a pass to the nurse's office. I think she keeps emergency toothbrushes next to the Band-Aid box . . . or I can always put a Band-Aid over my mouth.

"We're here," Mom says. "Please hand me your notebook so that I can write you a note."

I look in my pink knapsack and realize that I've left my notebook (with my homework in it) by my bed.

Mom and I rush into the school and explain why I'm late to the school secretary, who writes me a pass.

I walk down the hall, checking on my breath when no one's looking.

Walking into my classroom, I see that everyone is standing by Mrs. Holt's desk, talking to a kid who I don't know.

She's probably one of the kids who just moved into the new housing development.

Hal Henry was the first new kid in our class this year. Mrs. Holt has told us to expect more.

So I guess this person is one of them.

I look at her.

She's got brown hair, blue eyes, and she's not very skinny.

She looks like a perfectly nice new kid.

"She's here," Hannah Burton announces to the class in a voice that is much too sweet for the real Hannah Burton.

"AMBER BROWN has arrived . . . . . late, but here," Hannah says. "Let me be the one to introduce you two."

"Hannah, I can do that," Mrs. Holt says softly.

Hannah continues anyway: "AMBER BROWN . . . . . meet KELLY GREEN."

I start to smile and say hello and then it hits me.

The new person is named Kelly Green.

KELLY GREEN.

Chapter Five

I, Amber Brown, am flummoxed.

Flummoxed. Flummoxed. Flummoxed.

The other night, Max used that word, and when I asked what it meant, he helped me look it up in the dictionary.

It means confused and perplexed. (We looked that word up, too.)

I am so flummoxed.

How can there be another person in my class with a totally colorful name?

How much chance is there of two people with two names that are colors being in the same class?

I love having my unusual name.

There's a lot in my life that's changing.

My dad is moving back.

Mom and Max are going to get married.

I've been in the fourth grade only two months, and I had to get used to a new teacher, Mrs. Holt.

With all of the changes in my life, I would like for some things to stay the same.

My name is one of them. It's unusual. It's colorful. It's me, Amber Brown.

"Amber Brown. Kelly Green." Hannah Burton is smiling. "Let the Color Wars begin."

Hannah Burton is one of those people who is happiest when other people are unhappy, especially if she helps cause it.

If Hannah Burton were given a colorful name, it would be "Dirtball Mud."

The only war that I must deal with is the one that Hannah and I have. . . . It's a not very civil war. I don't want to be part of it,

but for some reason, Hannah is always saying disgusting, mean things.

Hannah Burton is a disgusting, mean thing, and I'm not going to let her start a fight that isn't even there between Kelly and me.

"Kelly Green." I look at Kelly and say, "It's really nice to meet you."

Mrs. Holt smiles and says, "Amber, I want you to be Kelly's special guide."

"I was hoping that I could be the guide." Hannah Burton is using her sweet voice. "After all, Amber has so much to do . . . . what with her having to devote so much extra time to getting organized."

And then Hannah Burton whispers something.

I think it's ". . . . and having to remember to brush her hair."

I put my hand to my hair and then remember that my teeth aren't brushed.

It's not my fault that Mom and I over-slept.

It just happens sometime to everyone.

Mrs. Holt looks at Hannah. "No, I really want Amber to show Kelly around . . . but I'm sure that there will be time for you, on your own, to talk with Kelly. It would be NICE of you to be helpful."

I, Amber Brown, swear that Mrs. Holt put extra emphasis on the word NICE.

It definitely would be nice if Hannah were nice.

I don't think Hannah Burton has a nice bone in her body.

Actually, she does have nice hair, though . . . . which she is always fluffing and telling everyone is so nice.

I run my fingers through my hair and then put my hand over my mouth to hide my morning breath, and I say, "I, Amber Brown, would love to show Kelly Green around the school."

Kelly smiles at me. "And I, Kelly Green, would love to have Amber Brown show me around the school."

Kelly Green not only has a colorful name, but she has just talked the way that I, Amber Brown, talk. That's a little weird.

I, Amber Brown, am the only one I know who says things like "I, Amber Brown." And I, Amber Brown, am getting a headache.

This is not a good day. I can't believe that so much stuff is happening. Oversleeping . . . . . not combing my hair . . . forgetting my homework.

This day is turning into a nightmare.

Maybe I'll get lucky and this will really be a nightmare.

Maybe I didn't oversleep this morning. Maybe I haven't gotten up yet, and this is all just a very bad dream.

I, Amber Brown, pinch myself really hard and hope that this is just a nightmare and that my mom will soon wake me up for real. And I won't have overslept. And I will have combed my hair. And I won't have morning mouth. And I won't have left my homework at home. And Kelly Green will only be part of a very bad dream.

The pinch hurts. It really hurts, really really hurts.

This is not a bad dream.

This is my life.

Chapter
Six

I, Amber Brown, am giving Kelly Green a minitour, the one from the classroom to the lunchroom.

She is telling me about herself. "I just love my parents. My daddy is a lawyer, and my mom is an accountant . . . . but she's staying home to take care of my little sister, Linda."

I'm glad that they didn't name her sister Lime . . . . Lime Green.

"And," she continues, "we have a new baby brother. He's so cute, and I help take care of him."

I ask her if his name is Oliver, Olive Green, for short.

She giggles. "No, silly. His name is Joey. Do you have brothers and sisters?"

"Nope," I say. "I'm an only child."

"That's so sad," Kelly says.

"I don't think so." I don't know why, but I want to step on Kelly's shoes, which look brand new. "I like being an only child."

I don't think Kelly should say that it's sad that I'm an only child.

I don't tell anyone that sometimes I do wish I had a younger brother or sister but that I don't think that's ever going to happen.

Next she tells me about her sheepdog.

I, Amber Brown, tell her that my mom is allergic to dogs . . . . and probably to sheep, too.

"Oh, that's so sad. Your mom would probably be allergic to our cat, Fluffy, too." She frowns.

I don't tell her that I think Fluffy is a stupid name for a cat.

I don't know why Kelly Green is annoying me, but she is. She's got two parents who are still together, a sheepish dog . . . . . . a fluffy cat . . . . . probably her brother and sister are fluffy, too. Her life sounds so perfect. . . . I bet she never oversleeps . . . or has morning mouth.

I bet she thinks her name is so perfect, too . . . but I don't.

I continue giving the tour to Kelly as we

walk to lunch. "And this is the nurse's office. If you don't mind, I need to stop here for a minute."

"Sure." Kelly giggles.

Kelly Green giggles a lot.

Sometimes I don't know why.

She just giggles.

I rush into the nurse's office and beg Mrs. McDowell for an "emergency toothbrush."

She hands me a package filled with a toothbrush and a tiny tube of toothpaste. She also hands me a comb.

Mrs. McDowell is prepared for any emergency.

I'm so glad that the PTA gives her some extra money so that she can buy stuff like this.

I rush into the bathroom and brush . . . . . and comb.

My teeth are so glad that she's got the toothbrush and toothpaste.

And I bet everyone who can smell my clean breath will be so glad.

My hair is also happy.

I come out of the bathroom and watch a little kid barf all over Mrs. McDowell's desk. It's the same kid who barfed when we had the skunk smell in our school.

I watch Kelly watch the kid barf, and then I watch Kelly barf.

The kid barfs again. . . . .

Oh, great. . . . . Ping-Pong barf.

The nightmare continues.

I, Amber Brown, don't barf, but this whole scene is making me feel pretty sick.

Mrs. McDowell is busy holding the little kid's head.

He's still barfing.

I just want to get out of there. I don't know what to do.

Kelly helps me decide. "You better go to lunch now, Amber. I guess I won't be having lunch after all. I think I have to go home. I always get sick when I see someone else get sick."

I look at her.

She's got barf dripping down her clothes and on her shoes.

Kelly Green is not giggling now.

I bet they were new clothes, because this is her first day of school here.

I, Amber Brown, feel bad for Kelly Green, but I'm glad that she's going home.

That'll give me another day to get used to her being in my class.

I leave the nurse's office, go into the cafeteria, buy my lunch, and go over to the table.

Brandi is saving two seats, one for me and one for Kelly.

I whisper to her and tell her what's happened.

"Wow," she says. "What a lousy way to start at a new school. I'm not even going to do a bulletin about this. It would only make her feel bad."

Brandi just moved here a year ago, so she always worries about new kids. She wants to become a television reporter, and practices by announcing news bulletins whenever she can.

Hal Henry comes over to our table. "Where's Kelly?"

Tiffani Shroeder looks at Hal. "Why? Do you want to ask her out?"

Hal blushes. "Get real. We're only in fourth grade. The only people you know who date are your Barbie and Ken dolls."

It's Tiffani's turn to blush. She hates it when someone teases her about her Barbie and Ken dolls.

Everyone does, though . . . . especially her little brother, who is always beheading her Barbies.

Hal explains: "She's my new next-door neighbor, and her mom makes the best cookies. She promised to give me some for lunch. So, why isn't she here? Did you give her an elevator pass and tell her to find the elevator?"

When Hal first got to the school, that's what one of the sixth-graders did to him.

Sometimes Hal Henry can be very gullible.

I tell him that Kelly's gone home, that she got sick from watching the little kid barf. "Kelly got so sick . . . her face turned green."

I think about what I've just said, and think it's kind of funny. Kelly's name is Green. Her face looked a little green . . . . and then very pale . . . . but first it looked green. Even her puke looked a little green. I wonder what she ate for breakfast.

Then I tell him how it was like Ping-Pong barf.

Hal laughs and then rushes off to tell everyone else what I've just told him.

"Kelly has turned really Green!"

Then I hear him say something about Ping-Pong barf, and all the boys laugh.

Brandi looks at me. "Amber."

"Yes?" I ask.

"That wasn't very nice." She frowns. "Now everyone is going to tease her."

I feel bad. I didn't mean to do anything that would make kids tease Kelly.

Sometimes I think Brandi worries too much and thinks that things are going to happen when they don't.

Part of me feels really bad.

I didn't mean to do something that would make trouble for Kelly and get her teased.

I, Amber Brown, know what it's like to be teased about a name.

However, I'm having a bad day.

And it's partly her fault.

So, can I help it if she's having a bad day, too?

I'm not the one who made her vomit.

I just told other people what happened.

Maybe now that they know, they'll send her a get-well card.

I give my lunch to Hal to make up for the cookie.

The lunch bell rings, and it's time to go back to class.

Mrs. Holt gives us an assignment to do a project about the Middle Ages. At first I think she's talking about people who are not young anymore and not yet old . . . . kind of like my parents and Max . . . . the middle ages.

But she explains that it's the Middle Ages, like in the olden days.

"By tomorrow I want you to turn in a paper explaining what your project is going to be."

Brandi whispers to me, "I'm going to phone Kelly when I go home, and give her the homework assignment."

I just hope they don't end up best friends and I'll be best friendless.

Mrs. Holt gives us a surprise quiz in math.

If she gives extra credit for erasing and

crossing out, then there's a chance that I passed the quiz. Otherwise, there's not much of a chance.

I lost my favorite good-luck pencil.

And then Brandi, Tiffani, Naomi, and I get detention for talking.

I already stay after school for Elementary Extension, because my mom can't pick me up until later. So, to make it a punishment, I have to go into a different room and just sit quietly, not able to do my homework or anything.

It's torture.

I, Amber Brown, have trouble sitting still and not doing anything.

Finally, it's time to go home.

Usually, it's my mom who picks me up, but today it's Brenda.

Maybe my day is finally getting better.

Chapter
Seven

Brenda and I hopscotch all the way home.

By the time we get to the front door, we're both exhausted.

Sitting down in the kitchen, we open up a box of chocolate-chip cookies.

Brenda says, "I'm so excited. Today, this guy that I've had a secret crush on asked me out."

"What's his name? What's he like?" I ask.

"His name is Ken, and he's really nice," she says.

"A real Ken doll." I giggle.

She pretends to bop me with the box of cookies. "He's cute and smart. He likes a lot of the things that I like. He's different in some ways, though. He dresses differently."

It makes me wonder what it means to Brenda when she says someone dresses differently. I hope that I meet this guy sometime.

"Brenda, I have a question." I smile at her.

"Yes?" She puts a cookie in her mouth.

"Do you think that you're ever going to cook for him?"

She laughs. "Are you trying to tell me that's not a good idea?"

I grin. "Maybe you should wait a couple of years until you feed him any of your Tuna Fish Delish."

Brenda laughs. "He can cook. He and his dad live alone . . . and I know that Ken can cook. That's one of the things that I like about him."

The phone rings.

It's my father.

He's calling all the way from Paris, France, just to talk to me.

He sounds so excited. "Amber, honey, I can't wait to move back and be closer to you. It's been so hard for me not to see you. We're going to make up for lost time. Just think, I'm returning very soon, and in just two weeks, we're going to be able to spend the weekend together."

"Oh, Daddy, that'll be so much fun." I, Amber Brown, am really excited, too.

It's been a long time since my dad and I have spent much time together.

"Amber," my dad continues, "just think . . . . it won't be long until we spend Thanksgiving together. Maybe we'll go into New York and watch them get ready for the Macy's parade."

"Oh, Dad, that sounds really great," I say, and then I remember. "Oh, no. Oh, oh. . . . Oh, no."

"Honey, what's wrong?" my father asks.

I am afraid to tell my father what I've just remembered, but I know that I have to tell him. "Dad, Mom and Max and I are going to Walla Walla. I can't spend Thanksgiving with you."

For a minute, there's no sound from him.

I just hold on to the phone, waiting for him to say something.

Finally, he speaks. "But I'll just be getting

back then. I was really looking forward to spending the holiday with you."

"Did you tell Mom that?" I bite on my bottom lip.

There's another silence.

My stomach starts to hurt.

He sighs. "No, I didn't. She didn't know. I just figured that I was coming back . . . . and that you and I could spend the time together. She's been able to be with you for all of the holidays since I left. I just assumed that we could be together for at least part of the time."

I don't know what to say.

I don't know what to do.

Because he moved to Paris, I've never had to deal with this before.

I just don't know what to say.

Max has already bought the tickets.

I wonder if there is a kind of a dream that is worse than a nightmare. Because that's what I'm having right now.

If I go to Walla Walla with Mom and Max, Dad's going to be unhappy.

If I stay here with Dad, Mom and Max are going to be unhappy.

Either way, I lose.

Either way, one of my parents loses.

At least, one of them wins.

But no matter what, I'm going to be the loser.

There's just no way there's going to be a "Thanks" in this Thanksgiving.

The only thing that I'm going to be thankful for is when it's over, and then it'll be Christmas and I'll have something else to worry about.

Chapter Eight

I, Amber Brown, think that life used to be so much easier.

I sit on my bed, looking at my "Countdown to Dad" book and at the "Dad Book," which I put together when he went away.

On the bed, I've got lots of other pictures. There's one of Mom and Max and me at the Jersey shore, pretending to be mermaids and a merman. There's the picture of the bowling team and Max, the coach. We're at the pizza party celebrating our "First Win in a Row." With the way our team is bowling, we may never have two wins in a row.

I, Amber Brown, don't know what to do.

Brenda knocks on the door and walks into my room.

"Are you all right?" she asks. "I thought you were in here doing your homework."

"I was going to do it. I just haven't gotten to it yet." I don't know what to say to Brenda.

It's like I have three parents, and she's got only one.

"Amber, I don't want to nag you," she says.

I, Amber Brown, realize that when someone says "I don't want to nag you," they're going to nag you.

And Brenda does. "Do your homework. You don't want to get into trouble with Mrs. Holt again for not doing it, do you?"

That's a lot of "Do"s about my homework . . . . . a lot of do-do.

I sigh. "Oh, OK."

Brenda says, "I'll go downstairs and finish

the dishes. And then I've got to study for a civics test. Call me if you need help."

I take out my notebook.

I've got to figure out a project on the Middle Ages.

I start planning.

The Middle Ages. . . . I don't want to do a stupid, boring research paper.

I'll do a newspaper instead . . . the kind that there would have been in the Middle Ages, if they could have had a newspaper.

I, Amber Brown, have to come up with a name for the paper.

Max reads *The New York Times*.

Aunt Pam reads the *Los Angeles Times*.

I'll call my paper *The Olden Times*.

And where *The New York Times* has written "All the news that's fit to print," I will put "All the news that fits, I'll print."

I start to list what will go in the paper.

There will be a news page about all of the stuff that's happening in the kingdom.

Then there will be a gossip column: "A Knight on the Town."

I'll have a travel section: "Whatever Floats Your Boat Across the Moat."

I'll draw the costumes and armor for the fashion section.

There will be a poetry page.

To show Mrs. Holt what the paper will be like, I write the first poem:

The Middle Ages
by Amber Brown

I could write pages about
   the Middle Ages.
It was a time when most
   animals didn't live in cages,
When there were myths
   about dragons in rages,
And there weren't a lot of
   people who were sages,
And most of the people
   didn't make very high wages.

It's not a great poem, but it's better than the one Bobby said in class the other day . . . "I'm a poet, but my toes don't show it."

There's a knock on the door.

This time it's my mom.

She gives me a kiss and then looks at my homework.

"Mom," I say, "I have something to tell you."

Then before I can tell her, I start to cry.

"Dad . . . . ." I sniffle.

"Is he all right?" She sounds worried.

"Dad called." I sniffle again.

"And?" she asks, holding my hand.

"And he wants to spend Thanksgiving with me." I look at her.

"Oh." She takes a deep breath. "For a minute, I thought it was something terrible."

I look at her.

She's being much calmer than I thought she would be.

I wonder if she still cares about my dad.

She thinks for about a minute, and then I can tell she realizes what it will mean to us . . . . and Walla Walla.

Trouble. Trouble.

I watch my mother's face. First she looks surprised, then angry, and then she bites her lip.

When my mother doesn't want to say something, she bites her lip.

She keeps her teeth on her lower lip for a long time.

Then she sighs. "Well, it isn't good, but at least no one is hurt . . . or sick or anything. It is terrible, though, for our plans."

"Mommy, what are we going to do? What am I going to do?" When I get upset, I call my mom "Mommy," even though it seems a little babyish.

She shakes her head. "I don't know, honey. I have to think about this before I say something that I'm going to regret later."

69

I just sit there.

She sighs.

Sometimes our family sighs a lot.

She gets up, gives me a kiss on the forehead, and says, "Give me a few minutes to think about this. I'll tell Brenda that she can leave now, and then I'll do some thinking and then come up here and talk to you."

She leaves.

I know that her "thinking" is going to have something to do with phone calls . . . . to my dad, to Max.

She goes downstairs.

I look at my homework, not able to work on it anymore.

"Amber, see you soon," Brenda yells up the stairs.

"'Bye for now," I yell back.

I just sit there and wait for my mother to come back.

She does.

I can tell that she's been crying from the

mascara on her face and how puffy her eyes are.

Mom sits down on my bed. "Amber, I've talked to your father. He really does want to see you. He thought we'd all be here and you could spend part of the vacation with each of us. I've tried to explain to him that we didn't do it intentionally . . . to take you

away just when he was returning . . . it's just that we've gotten used to his not being around. It may have been a mistake to plan this right now . . . but we didn't do it intentionally."

She's said that twice. I bet my father said that she did plan to do it, to cause trouble. I know she didn't. I was there.

Shaking her head, she says, "This is so like your father. He always waited 'til the last minute to make arrangements. It made me nuts then. It makes me nuts now. To say the least, it is SO annoying."

I don't want them to be mad at each other, to blame each other.

She pats my head. "Oh, honey, what do you want to do for Thanksgiving? Max and I have been talking, and we've decided that whatever you want to do, we'll go along with it. If you want us to cancel the trip, we will. If you want to stay with your father, we'll try to understand. If you want to go to Walla Walla, we will try to work that out."

I don't know what to do.

Why do I have to make the decision?

She says, "Your father and I have talked. He said that whatever you decide, he'll go along with. . . . He'll be very disappointed and sad, but he'll go along with it."

I shake my head. "I don't know."

Mom looks at me. "It's a tough decision, I know. That's why we've all decided to wait until your father comes back. Then you and he can talk . . . and you and I can talk . . . and then you and I and your father can all talk together."

That's going to be a lot of talking. . . . I don't know what's going to be said, but I do know that I'm the one who's got to make the decision.

I, Amber Brown, just don't know what to do.

Chapter Nine

Brandi's on her way.

We're not going to "paint the town red," but we are going to paint our fingernails all different colors.

We're going to Kelly Green's to do this.

I, Amber Brown, think that Kelly Green is terrific. She didn't even get mad at me when she got back after her "first day of school barf beginning," when all the kids teased her about turning green and some of the boys sang "Happy Barfday to You."

I, Amber Brown, think that while Kelly

Green is so nice, I, Amber Brown, was not so nice to her. It was my fault that Hal called her Kelly Greenbarf. Now some of the boys are calling her KGB, for Kelly Greenbarf.

I would feel totally bad and totally guilty about the way she's being teased about her barfday if I didn't really have so much on my mind.

I look down at my "Countdown to Dad" book, which I think should have been named "Countdown to Amber Brown's Nervous Breakdown."

Only four more days until my dad comes back, and I still don't know what I'm doing.

The doorbell rings.

"Amber, Brandi's here," my mother calls up the steps.

"Come on up," I yell.

Brandi rushes in. "Are you ready to go to Kelly's?"

Shaking my head, I sit down on the bed.

"Maybe I shouldn't go. I have to think about what I'm going to do."

Brandi sits down on the bed next to me. "Amber Marie Brown, you've done nothing but think about what to do. You're not having fun anymore. You're not fun anymore. Come on. We're going to have a great time. Kelly's bought all sorts of supplies . . . . polish, rhinestones, sparkles, glitter."

I look at Brandi. "Brandi Bonnie Colwin, I just don't know."

Tossing one of my stuffed animals at me, Brandi says, "Come on, Amber. You're going with me. You can't stay home all day and think about your problems."

"I guess I should go to Kelly's and think about my problems there." I grin and toss one of my stuffed animals at Brandi.

"Yes." Brandi stands up. "Let's go."

I sigh and get up. "Oh, all right. Wagons Ho."

"Wagons Ho" is something that Aunt Pam says when it's time to go somewhere. Saying that makes me think about the phone talk we had when I called her to beg her to take me for Thanksgiving. Even though she wouldn't "rescue" me, she said that I should remember that there is no one right or wrong answer to making the choice. She also said that it was a really tough situation to be in.

I'm really glad that she told me that.

"Get your nail polish." Brandi tugs at my arm. "Kelly is waiting."

Going over to my dresser, I go into the top drawer, and pull out my one nail polish.

It's light pink. It's "Barbie." It's all dried out. It was a gift from Tiffani Shroeder for my fifth birthday.

I, Amber Brown, don't usually wear

makeup unless it is for Halloween or unless it's for a special occasion, like when I went to a slumber party and we all made ourselves up.

"Yuck. Yuck. Yuckoid. Is that all you have?" Brandi asks.

I grin. "Brenda . . . the Amber-sitter . . . to the rescue. Look at what she loaned me."

I pull a little paper bag out of the bureau and empty the contents.

"Wow. That's awesome." Brandi looks through them. "Color Me Cantaloupe. Tangerine. Melon. Candy Apple Red. . . . Does Brenda put these on her nails, or does she eat them?"

"Silly," I say, "of course she doesn't eat them."

Brandy grins at me. "But they're all named food colors."

I grin back. "But they're liquid. She drinks them."

"Yag." Brandi clutches her throat.

We both pretend to drink from the bottles.

Then we pretend to choke.

And then we fall down on the floor.

The phone rings.

I, Amber Brown, used to like it when the phone rang . . . . especially if it was a call for me.

Now I hate it.

I'm always afraid that it's my dad or Max . . . . and that they are going to want to talk to me. They don't even mention Thanksgiving. They are just so nice that it makes me feel bad, because I know that one of them is going to feel bad when I make my choice.

All of this niceness is driving me crazy.

"Amber, it's for you," my mother calls up.

I know that Mom is going to feel bad if I don't choose her and Max.

"It's Kelly," she says.

I let out my breath.

It was almost as if I had stopped breathing for a second . . . . and that wasn't because I was choking from pretend-drinking the nail polish.

I pick up the phone.

"Where are you?" Kelly asks, and then giggles. "Well, actually, now I know WHERE you are . . . . THERE . . . . . but why aren't you WHERE you are supposed to be . . . . HERE?"

I say, "It's my fault. We'll be there soon."

I, Amber Brown, am starting to feel guilty that I made us late for going over to Kelly's.

I, Amber Brown, am feeling guilty a lot lately.

It should be a nail polish color . . . . Amber Brown Gilt.

We rush downstairs.

Since we are so late, my mom says, "I'll drive you over to Kelly's."

I know that my mom is being nice to do that.

I also know that she likes to see where I'm going to be when she doesn't know the people I'm going to visit.

I think that's a Mom kind of thing to do.

I wonder what my dad's going to be like when he gets back.

I wonder if he'll check everything out the way Mom does.

When they were married, Mom always did those things.

I wish I didn't keep thinking about all of this.

I wish I could just think of the fun that I'm having with Brandi and the fun that I think we're going to have at Kelly Green's, unless Kelly is going to do something to get back at me for telling everyone that she barfed.

I, Amber Brown, am turning into a major worrier.

I, Amber Brown, have a lot to worry about.

I, Amber Brown, wonder if Kelly has a nail polish named Kelly Greenbarf.

I, Amber Brown, am going to try to have fun when we get to Kelly's.

Chapter Ten

One of my fingernails falls off.

I catch it before it hits the carpet.

It's a great save.

Since Kelly's house is brand new, the carpet is also brand new.

I, Amber Brown, would hate to be the first one to get the carpet dirty.

If we were doing our own nails, I wouldn't have to worry. My real nails don't fall off. The false fingernails do. But my own nails have been so bitten down that there would be no room for all the stuff that we have to put on them ...... nail polish, glitter, rhinestones, decals, silver and gold strips, tiny metal stars, and diamonds. Using the false nails is good because there's room to decorate them, and they can come off and on.

"Look." Brandi shows us her thumbnail.

It's light blue with a rose decal in the middle, and on the left are three dark blue rhinestones.

Kelly's sheepdog, Darth Vader, comes over.

He looks like a gigantic hair ball.

Putting his chin on my knee, he slobbers all over my jeans.

Gross.

I don't know what to do.

One of my hands has newly painted nails on it.

The other hand is holding the nail polish brush.

Darth Vader slobbers more, and then he sneezes and gunk comes out of his nose.

My knee is not a pretty sight.

"I think he likes you." Kelly giggles.

I, Amber Brown, look at the slobber and snot on my leg and wish that Darth Vader liked me less.

I wiggle my knee to try to get him to move.

He just stays there and starts to wag his tail, which hits my other leg.

I wiggle.

He wags.

I wiggle again.

He wags . . . . and then he slobbers again.

Darth Vader and I stare at each other for a minute.

I blink first . . . . . at least I think I blink first. It's hard to tell, with all that hair in front of his eyes.

"Let's paint his nails," I say.

Kelly, Brandi, and I look at each other and laugh.

"We could do each one a different color."

We look at his feet.

There's a lot of hair on them.

Kelly rushes up to her bedroom, and returns with lots of little barrettes.

We pin back the hair around his toes, and then Kelly holds him down.

Brandi holds out the nail polish bottle.

I kneel down and paint one of his nails Candy Apple Red.

For the next one I use Perfectly Peach.

He starts to lick his nails, so Kelly holds onto his head.

When I finish painting all ten of Darth Vader's toenails different colors, Brandi and I lie down on the floor and blow on his toes to help them dry faster.

He slobbers on my head, so when I'm blowing on his nails, I spit on one to get even.

He licks the top of my head.

I, Amber Brown, will definitely have to take a shower when I get home.

We spray his toenails with quick-dry liquid and then start working on our own nails. Darth Vader sits down beside me, chewing on the barrettes that are still on his feet.

Darth Vader is a little weird, but if I ever got a dog, I think one like Darth Vader would be terrific, only smaller and less drooly. I know that there are big poodles and there are tiny poodles (which are called toy poodles). I wonder if there are such animals as toy sheepdogs. With my mom allergic to dogs, though, the only kind of dog that I've ever been able to get is one that is a toy. I wonder if my dad will let me get a dog when he moves back. I wonder who would take care of it while I'm at my mom's. I wonder if he would take care of it, feed it, and walk it . . . and I, Amber Brown, could just play with it.

Thinking about this reminds me of my worries, but right now I'm having a good time. I'm glad that Brandi made me come. I'm glad that Kelly is so nice.

"Ooops." Kelly's nail falls off her thumb and lands on the floor.

She picks it up.

There's carpet lint on it . . . . . and on the carpet is a spot of Shimmer Glitter Mauve.

"Ooops," Kelly says again.

We all look down at the carpet and then at each other.

"Ooops," we all say.

Kelly's mother walks into the room and puts a plate of cookies on the table. "What is all this 'ooopsing' about?"

Kelly swallows hard and then says, "Mom, it was an accident."

"You know that is one of my least favorite sentences," Mrs. Green says. "What's the accident?"

Kelly points with one of her Shimmer

Glitter Mauve fingernails. "Polish on the rug."

Mrs. Green does not look happy.

She looks at the spot, saying nothing for a minute, then she sighs and reaches for the bottle of nail-polish remover and a cotton pad.

We all sit quietly and watch as she tries to clean up the spot.

I think . . . . . . Please, oh please . . . . . Out, darn spot. . . .

Kelly, Brandi, and I look at one another.

I cross my fingers, getting nail polish on my hand.

The polish comes off the rug.

I, Amber Brown, am so relieved. I hate it when kids are having fun and something happens that ruins everything and makes a grown-up angry.

"Be careful, now," Mrs. Green says.

We promise to be careful.

Mrs. Green leaves, and then returns with

trash bags to spread out on floor under us.

When Darth Vader moves so that she can put the bags down, the barrettes clink against each other.

Mrs. Green looks at him.

Then she looks at us.

Kelly shrugs. "We decided it would be quite a feat to do his nails."

I, Amber Brown, wonder if she means "feat" or "feet."

Mrs. Green laughs. "Your father refers to that dog as his first son. I'm not sure what he's going to say when he sees his dog. I'll just tell him that it's the paws that refreshes."

She laughs again.

I, Amber Brown, don't get what she means by the paws refreshing. . . . But there are a lot of things grown-ups say that I don't get.

Mrs. Green keeps smiling, and says, "Just wait 'til your father gets home."

That is something that I, Amber Brown, do understand.

Just wait 'til your father gets home. . . . . . . Kelly doesn't look too upset about her father's return.

Now I, Amber Brown, just have to wait 'til my father comes home.

Chapter Eleven

It's so weird.

It feels like everything in my life is changing, but some things don't.

I still have to go to school.

And I still have to sit through reports as if everything is normal.

Jimmy Russell and Bobby Clifford get up to give their reports.

I, Amber Brown, can't believe that Mrs. Holt let them be a team. They goof around so much.

"We are the Billington brothers," Jimmy

Russell and Bobby Clifford say at exactly the same time.

"I am John, and I was seven when the *Mayflower* came over to America," Jimmy says. "And I almost blew up the *Mayflower* with gunpowder when it got to Plymouth."

It's obvious that Jimmy likes the character he is playing.

"And I am Francis, and I was nine. Dur-

ing our first winter in Massachusetts, I climbed a tree and saw a lot of water. I thought it was the Pacific, but it was a large pond."

"Duh," Hal Henry calls out.

"Quiet," Mrs. Holt says.

Bobby says, "Yeah, quiet. . . . They named the pond 'Billington Sea.'"

"Double duh," Hal says quietly.

Then Bobby and Jimmy tell how the Billingtons were TROUBLE. . . . How John got lost in the woods for days, and how the Indians found him and helped him return. How their father was so bad that he was one of the few people arrested during the Pilgrims' first year in America because he wouldn't stand watch . . . and how he was hanged nine years later because he killed someone.

Now this is interesting Thanksgiving information, I think. How come no one ever told us all of this before?

I look at Bobby and Jimmy.

This is such a great report they are giving that I wonder if they are telling the truth.

I look at Mrs. Holt to see if she's going to yell at them for making this all up, but she doesn't. In fact, when they are finished, she tells them what a good job they did.

Then she tells us how the Pilgrims who were going to the "New World" for religious reasons called themselves the "Saints" and all the others the "Strangers." She says the Billingtons were part of the "Strangers" group.

That explains why Billy and Jimmy did such a good job. . . . They are a little strange themselves.

I'm not sure I like the way the Pilgrims labeled the people who weren't them.

Next, Hannah Burton and Hal Henry get up.

"I am a Pilgrim mother," she says.

"I am a Pilgrim father," Hal says.

I, Amber Brown, think that these two Pilgrims are definitely not "Saints" . . . . . . that both of them are "Strangers."

Pilgrim mothers . . . . . .

Pilgrim fathers . . . .

I start thinking about my own mother and father.

I feel more like a Pilgrim turkey than a Pilgrim child. . . . And if I can't decide what I am going to do this Thanksgiving, my goose is cooked.

I think about it. . . . How can a turkey think about having a goose that is cooked? What does it really mean to have a goose cooked? Max is always saying that when we are watching television and someone gets into trouble. "His goose is cooked" is what he always says. And why do people call other people "turkeys"? I also wonder if someone could goose a turkey. These are a few of the things that I think about while I should be listening to the report.

I kind of giggle when I think about someone goosing a turkey. Maybe that's what it's called when my mother goes into the turkey and pulls out one of those plastic bags filled with turkey parts, like the gizzard and liver and heart and whatever. She says that the first Thanksgiving dinner she cooked, she didn't know that it was in there, so she cooked the bird with the bag still inside, mixed in with the stuffing.

I wonder what the real first Thanksgiving would have been like if a Pilgrim mother had done something like that. Probably they didn't have plastic bags then, though.

I wonder what's going to happen if Mrs. Holt realizes that I'm not paying attention to the report.

Maybe if I paid attention to the report, I would find out more about geese and turkeys, but I, Amber Brown, have a lot on my mind.

Tonight's the night that my father gets back to America.

I look over at the clock on the wall to see how many hours until his plane arrives.

Five more hours . . . . and then he has to go through customs, rent a car, leave the airport, and go to the Donaldsons' house, where he is going to stay until he finds an apartment.

The Donaldsons used to be friends of my parents, until my parents got a divorce. . . . But after the divorce they were just friends of my dad's. Mom says that in the divorce settlement, he got custody of the Donaldsons. She's kidding, I think.

I look at the clock again. Four hours and fifty-three minutes until he is in America. . . . And then, as soon as he can, he'll come over to our house. He and I get to go out to dinner. Then we'll come back home, and he and Mom and I will talk.

I can't wait.

I look at the clock again.

This time, Mrs. Holt is standing under the clock and looking at me.

Quickly, I look back at the Pilgrim father and mother, Hal and Hannah.

I use the Amber Brown technique of looking interested even when I'm not.

I pick out something on their faces that I can stare at.

Hal has a little scar above his left eyebrow.

Hannah has a milk mustache.

I am so glad that Hannah has a milk mustache and that no one told her before her report.

I stare first at the scar and then at the mustache.

That way I look very interested.

Sometimes I make a little nod so that it looks like I'm thinking about what has been said.

I only hope that Mrs. Holt doesn't give us a quiz on this as soon as the report is over.

She doesn't.

Hannah hands out a list of the real Thanksgiving Day menu, reminding us that it was cooked by four women.

Hal hands out a list of all the known people at the first Thanksgiving Day dinner.

It's kind of weird.

Mrs. Holt says that it wasn't even called Thanksgiving Day when it first happened ... and she gives us a lot of the real facts.

This would be very interesting if I didn't have so much on my mind.

The only fact that I really want to know is which parent I spend Thanksgiving Day with this year.

And no one else in the world has the answer to that but me.

And I, Amber Brown, don't have that answer yet.

Chapter
Twelve

My dad is late.

My dad is very late.

I, Amber Brown, am going nuts because it's almost eight o'clock and he's still not here.

My mom and I sit at the kitchen table, waiting for him and doing my "Book Report in a Bag."

Actually, I'm doing the report and she's supervising, but I'm having trouble concentrating.

Now it's eight twenty-two, and my dad's still not here.

I'm all ready. I've got on my basic black leggings and one of the sweatshirts that he sent me, the one that says "I love Paris" in French. I'm also wearing a scrunchie that my Aunt Pam sent me. Some people might say it's a little babyish, but I still love it. There are two round globes, and in each of them are all different colored jacks. It's so "fun,"

and I love the way they move when I turn my head.

I hate that he's late.

It's not his fault that he's not here yet.

It's really not anyone's fault.

I, Amber Brown, don't care that it's not anyone's fault.

I just want him to be here.

He called the second that he could, once he got off the plane and to a phone.

The plane in Paris didn't take off on time because of equipment trouble, and then there was a backup at Newark airport.

Mom says that I should just be happy that Dad got back safely. She's right, but I'm very disappointed that he's not here and that the plans have changed.

I really wanted to go out to dinner, just me and my dad. We were going to talk about everything and then come back to the house, and then Mom and Dad and I would talk. Now it's just going to be THE TALK, and I'm not sure how much fun that's going to be.

I just wanted my dad to get back safely . . . . . and on time.

He and Mom and I have to make THE BIG DECISION, because there are only a few days until Thanksgiving and plans have to be made.

I, Amber Brown, still don't know which parent I'm going to be with for the Thanksgiving vacation.

"Let's practice your book report," my mom says. "Amber, I don't want what's happening to affect your schoolwork."

"I got an A on my Middle Ages report," I remind her.

She smiles. "I know. I'm very proud of you."

I like it . . . . I like it a lot . . . . when Mom says that she's very proud of me.

I think about all of the times she's helped me with my homework.

My dad used to help me, too, before the divorce and before he moved to Paris.

I bet he'll help me now that he's back.

I hope that he'll be proud of me, too.

I wonder if they'll both be proud of me when I make my decision.

I, Amber Brown, am getting so tired of thinking about all of this over and over again.

Starting my report, I turn my head, and the balls with the jacks in them make a clinky sound. I like that sound. My "Book Report in a Bag" is on *The Watsons Go to Birmingham—1963,* by Christopher Paul Curtis.

I hold up the brown paper bag that groceries came in. On the front, I've drawn a picture from the book. It's of the Watsons, the mom and dad and the two brothers and the sister, in the car. The two brothers are in the backseat fighting with each other, and

the parents are in the front seat being driven crazy by the brothers while they are driving from Detroit, Michigan, to Birmingham, Alabama.

I pull objects out of the bag to explain the book. Paper dolls of the Watsons . . . . . I pretend to have the characters talk to each other. The mother is saying to one of the boys, "I think that it's time for you to stay with your grandmother for a while, until you learn to be good."

Then I pull out a copy of a newspaper headline about civil rights from the 1960s, explaining what the country was like, what it might have been like for some black families during that time.

And then I take out the little church that I borrowed from Kelly's dad's train set . . . . and explain how four girls were killed when someone set off a bomb in the Birmingham church. I tell about how they were only a few years older than the people in my class.

I say, "Look around the class and think about what it would be like if, all of a sudden, four of us were killed because of prejudice, because some people didn't like our color."

I end the report by saying, "This is a very

funny and sad book, and I love it, and I think that everyone should read it."

My mother applauds and says, "Good job. May I borrow the book?"

I nod. "It's from the library. So I'll renew it, and then you can read it."

The doorbell rings.

I jump up.

I can't wait to see him.

I hope that he likes the way I look.

The doorbell rings again.

"We're coming. Hold on." My mom does not sound as happy as I feel.

I open the door.

It's my dad.

I jump up into his arms.

"Ooph," he says.

Maybe I'm going to have to stop doing that now that I'm in the fourth grade. It's just that I was always able to do that when I was in the second grade, which was the last time he really lived in this house.

He looks over at my mother and nods. "Sarah."

"Philip," she answers.

Their voices are very cold.

But they're not fighting with each other. Not yet.

Maybe they won't fight with each other anymore.

I give my dad a kiss on his balding head and get down.

We all just stand there for a minute.

And then my mother says, "Let's go into the living room and talk."

"I was hoping that we could go out and get something to eat," Dad says. "I haven't had a chance to have dinner. I rushed right over here as soon as I dropped off my bags."

Mom looks at her watch. "No, sorry. It's a school night."

For a minute, it looks like Dad is going to say something, to disagree, and then he repeats, "It's a school night."

"Mom," I beg.

My mom looks at him and then at me. "We have some leftovers from dinner. I suppose that while we're talking, I can feed you."

"It'll be like old times." My dad smiles a funny smile.

"Let's hope not." My mom lifts an eyebrow.

As we walk into the kitchen, my dad and I hold hands.

I hope that Mom doesn't mind that I'm holding hands with Dad and not with her.

It's so weird.

We're all in the house together.

I wish it was like old times, the old times that were good.

At least that way I wouldn't still have to make this awful decision.

But I don't think that's going to happen. . . .

Chapter
Thirteen

A decision is a decision is a decision.

And I, Amber Brown, have made my decision.

It is the second-hardest thing I've ever had to do in my entire life.

The first-hardest is the thing that I have to do next.

That will be telling my parents what my decision is.

I, Amber Brown, wish that I could just write that decision on a piece of paper, leave the room while they read it, and then when I come back in, have everything be OK. I wish that no one's feelings would get hurt. But it's not going to work that way.

I must make the announcement.

I'm only nine years old, in the fourth grade.

Why do I have to do this?

I know the answer to that. I have to make the choice because I have no choice.

Sometimes life is confusing.

Sometimes it's not easy.

This is one of those times when it's both . . . confusing and not easy.

The only thing that came close to being this hard was having to say good-bye to my best friend, Justin, when he moved to Alabama.

This is a bazillion times harder than Justin's good-bye, and that was absolutely, totally, and terribly awful.

"Mom, Dad," I say, "I, Amber Brown, am spending Thanksgiving with Dad."

My dad claps his hands.

My mom looks like she's going to cry.

They both look at me, and then they look at each other.

My dad's smiling, but he's not gloating, like "Ha-ha. I won."

He quietly says, "Sarah, Amber will stay with you Christmas Eve and Christmas Day."

My mom looks at him. "That's what WE decided, that whomever Amber didn't get to be with at Thanksgiving, she would be with at Christmas."

I almost ask if they've worked out who I will be with on Groundhog Day, but I don't.

Mom looks very sad, but not very mad, which was what I was afraid would happen.

I figure that I have to say something. "It's not that I love one of you more than the other . . . but, Mom, you and Max have each other. Dad has no one. He's just moved back."

She knows that's true, that he's got a few friends left over from when he used to live here, but all of them are busy with their own families on Thanksgiving.

I am my dad's own family.

So I am staying with him.

"I can pick Amber up at school on Tuesday, and then we can go directly into the city," my father says.

"You can pick her up here," Mom says.

"I will feel much better knowing that she's with you . . . . not waiting at the school because you got delayed at a business meeting or something."

My dad looks angry, but he bites his lip.

"Philip, you would do the same if you were me. I would worry. . . . . Amber is the most important thing in my life."

"Mine, too," my dad says.

I feel wonderful that they both are saying that.

I have something to say, though. "Hey . . . . . I'm not a thing. I'm a person."

"We know that, honey," my mom says.

I can see that there are tears in her eyes, tears that are close to rolling down her face.

This is definitely not fair.

I, Amber Brown, feel bad, though.

In fact, I feel really bad.

I want to go to Walla Walla with Mom and Max.

And I want to go to New York City with my dad.

And I want my parents to get back together.

And I want Mom and Max always to be friends and do things together.

I want to make choices and not feel guilty.

I want to not have to make choices, not ones like this.

The ones I want to make are things like . . . . . Should I have chocolate or vanilla ice cream? If I get a new bike, how many speeds should it have? Should my allowance be raised? Should I have to do homework, or not have to do homework?

Now, these are good choices for a kid to make . . . not the ones that I have to make . . . choosing one parent instead of the other.

"OK." My mother sighs and stands up. "Philip, I'll have Amber ready to be picked up here at three-thirty. Her bags will be packed. Just let us know what kind of clothes she'll need . . . and write down all the information I'll need . . . where to contact you, what the phone number is . . . and I'll give you the same."

All of a sudden, my life has gotten much more involved . . . much more organized.

My father stands up. "OK."

When my mother picks up the dishes to put in the dishwasher, my father offers to do it.

She shakes her head. "No, Philip, you are a guest in my home. I'll do it."

They look at each other.

I bet they are thinking about when he wasn't a guest in her home, when this was his home, too.

They must be thinking about that because I, Amber Brown, am.

"Thank you, Sarah," he says. "Thank you for everything."

While she is putting the dishes away, I walk Dad out to the living room and to the door.

He leans downs and gives me a hug. "Amber, I am so happy that we are going to be spending Thanksgiving together."

I just stand there.

He says, "You feel bad that you're not going to be able to spend Thanksgiving with your mom, right?"

I nod.

"I can understand that." He looks at me. "Would you rather go with Mom? I want you to do what you want to do, not what you think you should."

"Dad," I say, "I made my decision. I don't want to think about it anymore. What I wanted was not to have to decide . . . but I did . . . because you and Mom made the decision to get divorced, to not be a family anymore."

"Maybe that's why I want you to think about it before *your* decision is final," he says.

I try to figure out what he means by what he's just said. Does that mean that he's sorry he and Mom got divorced? Does it just mean that he knows it's important to make the right decision, because being divorced has been good?

Grown-ups. Grown-ups who are parents. Grown-ups who are *my parents*. . . . It's all very confusing.

I think about what Justin once said. . . .

You can pick your friends. You can pick your nose . . . but you can't pick your friends' noses. . . .

Well, I didn't get to pick my parents.

I am glad that I have them, though.

I just wish that I wouldn't have to spend the rest of my life picking one of them and not the other.

Chapter Fourteen

Dear Justin,

Guess what??????!!!!!!!!!!!

My dad's moved back from Paris.

You probably already knew that, because my mom tells your mom everything.

I'm glad our moms are still best friends and phone each other all the time and write each other.

Thanks for sending the picture of you at Halloween. (I know that your mom was the one who sent the picture, but I love the way that you wrote on it. . . . . "I am Dracula . . . and I want to bite your neck . . .

but I'd probably get rabies.")

My dad and I went to New York for Thanksgiving.

It was sooooooooooooooooooooooooooooooooooooo fun.

We stayed at a hotel. (They had mail chutes on each floor. It was soooooo cool to watch as the mail went down . . . . . the chutes were glass. One morning I saw a pancake going down. I don't want to think what the mail looked like when that splattered on it.)

On Thanksgiving Eve, we went over to the American Museum of Natural History. . . . . Oh, Justin, it was sooooooooooooooooo fun. I wish that you had been there. It's called "Inflation Night," and on either side of the museum, people were blowing up

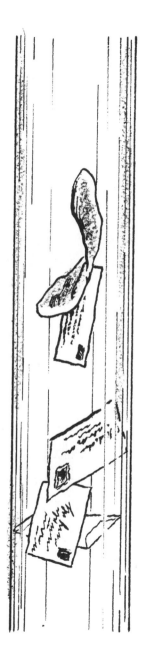

the balloons that are in the parade. I heard someone say, "Just think of Barney as half full instead of half empty."

You should have seen that stupid purple dinosaur. Parts of it looked gigantic, and parts of it looked like it had liposuction . . . you know, when doctors get fat out of a person's body . . . well, this looked like a definite case of dinosuction.

While we were walking around, we met some people that my dad used to work with before he moved to Paris. They are the Fagerstroms. They live in Texas and were just visiting for the holiday. The mom and dad are Terry and Marie . . . and they have three kids, Ian, EmmaLee, and Eli.

We all went to dinner at the Museum Cafe. The kids all teased me and said that I "talk funny." I think that I, Amber Brown, talk absolutely New Jersey Normal . . . and they are the ones that talk funny. I kept calling Eli, who is three, "cowpoke" and

kept poking him. He poked back. Once he accidentally poked me in the nose . . . . and Dad said I was "poker faced." And then all of the grown-ups laughed. I just hate it when they make jokes I don't understand.

It was really late when we finished dinner, and Dad and I went back to the hotel.

In the morning, we went to the parade. It was so fun . . . . the balloons . . . . the floats . . . . the little nerdlets crying because some grown-ups cut in front of them. I kept looking at the television cameras and waving. I kept hoping that you and your family were watching.

Afterward we went out to a great restaurant, Little Jezebel's, for Thanksgiving lunch. Then I called Mom . . . and Max. It was only breakfast time in Walla Walla, and they were having pancakes with syrup for breakfast. But no mail!

It sounded like they were having an OK

time . . . but that they missed me. And that made me feel sad.

Mom told me not to feel blue. Just to have a good time and we'd all be together at Christmas.

Before I had a chance to think about what she'd said, she told me, "We all . . . that means you and I and Max. After Christmas you'll be seeing your dad again."

Anyway, I hope that you had fun over Thanksgiving. Your mom told mine that you like your Dracula costume so much that you were thinking of wearing it at Thanksgiving . . . a Pilgrim vampire. You know that if you had come over on the *Mayflower*, you probably wouldn't have been a Pilgrim. They said that they were "Saints." You definitely would have been a "Stranger."

If you are still a vampire, don't forget to leave deposits at the blood bank.

Your friend,

Amber Brown

P.S. Justin . . . . guess what now? I'm your friend . . . . but since you're Dracula . . . . I guess you're my fiend. . . . What a difference an "r" makes.

P.P.S. Speaking of "r's" and letters, are you going to WRITE BACK SOON!!!!!!!!!!!!!!!!! !!!???????!!!!!!

P.P.P.S. I've made you a little scrapbook of what my Thanksgiving was like. Maybe next year you and your family can go to the parade with me and whichever parent I'm with. Justin . . . . you are sooooooooo lucky

that your parents are still together and that they still love each other.

I wish that mine did.

But then if they did, I wouldn't know Max . . . . I wouldn't have two places that I'm going to live . . . . I wouldn't be Amber Brown the way I am now.

It's OK. . . . Sometimes I feel blue, sometimes I see red, sometimes I'm green with envy. . . .

I'm Amber Brown . . . . and I guess I'm just always going to have a colorful life.